Janey's Own

LATTER-DAY DAUGHTERS

BOOKS IN THE LATTER-DAY DAUGHTERS SERIES

Janey's Own

LATTER-DAY DAUGHTERS

Launi K. Anderson

Published by
Deseret Book Company
Salt Lake City, Utah

To Brother and Sister Day, of the
Manchester Ward, Los Angeles, California
June 10, 1978
The Kirbys thought of you, and
whispered prayers of gratitude

Library of Congress Cataloging-in-Publication Data

Anderson, Launi K., 1958–
   Janey's own / by Launi K. Anderson.
     p.   cm. — (The Latter-day daughters series)
   Summary: When Janey's father, hated for being an abolitionist and
Mormon, goes away on business, greedy relatives plan to claim her
family's plantation and sell the black servants as slaves.
   ISBN 1-57345-319-6 (pbk.)
   [1. Fathers and daughters—Fiction. 2. Slavery—Fiction.
3. Mormons—Fiction. 4. Afro-Americans—Fictions.] I. Title.
II. Series.
PZ7.A54375Jan   1997
[Fic]—dc21   97-37259
                                                CIP
                                                AC

Printed in the United States of America   8006

10   9   8   7   6   5   4   3   2   1

"In the end, all that really matters is how we have treated each other."

MARVIN J. ASHTON

CONTENTS

CHAPTER ONE

Yesterday's Shadows

Mammy* pulled the boar brush* down to the end of my hair in quick strokes.  Though her large hand held tight to the top of my head, there seemed no earthly way for me to keep from bobbing forward with each tug. I learned in my twelve years that more hair stayed attached to my head if I sat very still and kept the fussing to myself.

"Child," she said, "haven't I always held on to you so's you don't be runnin' wild like the devil himself?"

"Yes, Mammy."

See the glossary at the end of this book for an explanation of unusual words and expressions marked with an asterisk (*).

"And don't I tie a bonnet on your head whenever you go out in the wind?"

I sighed. "Yes, Mammy."

"And don't I brush you out each night before you sleep?"

"Yes, Mamm . . ."

"Then tell me, child, where all these knots come from? I be working till sundown gettin' this mess out."

Mammy had to know she wasn't scaring me. I'd been listening to her playful scolding all my life. I just pretended not to notice.

Society,* which my dear Mammy wants me suitable for, holds that a young lady has no business thinking for herself, or doing anything fun, exciting, or at all useful. Especially if you could possibly wrinkle something in the meantime. If I was a perfect Southern lady, why, my hair would know how to behave properly. Trouble is, only half of my mind is interested in being proper. The other half dreams of adventure, riding hard, or getting truly dirty once in a while.

At least Papa understands. He says, "Everyone

should have the right to decide what this life holds for them."

Papa, being a fine horseman, likes nothing better than an evening ride through the country. Since Momma had always been too much of a lady for such things, he taught me to ride very young. Even though Mammy thought it improper, we loved to race through the meadows anyway. We just had to make sure to do it when she wasn't looking. There was no way to hide what it did to my hair, but I don't care. A person can go crazy being ladylike all the time.

Working my fingertips over the lace at my neck, I considered the questions stirring around in my mind.

"Mammy?" I said.

"Hmmm?"

"What do you think *secede* means?"

"Secede? Why you thinkin' about that?"

"No real reason," I fibbed. "Just wondering. So what does it mean?"

She slid her hand down and took hold of all my hair at once and worked on it like she was scrubbing the main hall floor.

"Well, I hear Massa* say it be if one state don't like being part of America, they just decide to be their own country. That's secedin'. But Massa say it ain't gonna happen to this here land. So put it out of your head."

"It doesn't sound so bad," I said.

"'Less you be the president and you be needin' to keep the people together. How you suppose he'd like seeing everyone goin' off to start they own country? Why, he wake up one mornin' to find he's all alone with no one to be president of."

I'd have been smarter to save some curiosity for another day, but seeing how well the first question went gave me courage.

"Well, then," I said, "what is an abolitionist?"*

She tightened her grip and pulled my head back to where I could almost see her looking down at me. Reaching to rub my sore scalp, I thought, *Yes, I should've waited.*

"Miss Jane, where you gettin' these words from?"

I turned carefully and took the brush from her. It was already so full of my own hair, I couldn't risk leaving the weapon unguarded.

"Cousin Leanna says . . ."

Mammy slapped her hands down hard onto her round hips and stared directly into my eyes.

"And what you listening to that cousin Leanna for? She just loves gettin' you all worked up. You know yourself she's full of a polecat's meanness.* Child, don't never be taking her words for truth. Now, you just go and . . ."

"Mammy, listen to me. Leanna says that abolitionists are evil, wicked demons that carry away slaves in the night. Then they are sold into the Deep South* or taken away to Canada. And everyone knows that Canadians are cannibals."*

Mammy sputtered and twisted her face.

"One thing is certain," I said, slowing down to say each word by itself. "They . . . are . . . never . . . seen . . . again. Do you think it's true, Mammy?"

She was still scowling at me, but I knew she was getting ready to say something, because her hands came off her hips and crossed tight over her chest.

"Missy Jane, what would your papa say of you asking all this? You gonna get me into trouble."

"No, I won't, Mammy. My papa trusts you. Why, you've always taken the very best care of me. Besides, he wants people to learn all they can so their lives will be rich and full. I'd ask him straight out, but he tries too hard to keep the real world from coming near me." Imitating my father, I cleared my throat and said low, 'Don't go filling your pretty head with all these adult concerns.'"

Mistake number two. Mammy's mouth got all persimmon-puckered,* and she came so close up to my face that I backed right onto the bed. Mammy has never been one to hold herself in,* so I figured it wise to take what was coming.

"Don't you go bad-mouthing your papa now," she said. "I won't stand for it. You hear me? He's the best, most kind-hearted massa to walk this earth.

"Child, he wrote every one of us up they own freedom paper* years ago. Said we be free. But what we goin' do? Leave? Go where? Since he married your momma—rest her soul—there ain't nobody, man nor beast, that been sorely done to* here. Only five slaves took them papers and went off. The rest of us—well, we stayed. We take care of y'all and your papa takes care of us. We like it that way. So you just better not be saying nothing 'bout my massa."

She kept mumbling under her breath, letting just a word or two slip out louder than the rest. " . . . hush up . . . talking . . . my massa . . . child . . . know nothin' . . ."

Trying to ease her up a bit, I said, "I know. You're right, of course. It's just not so difficult to get an answer from you, that's all."

She closed her eyes for a long minute, like I was trying her soul.

"Please?" I said, batting my lashes at her.

"Missy, that don't work with me," she said.

Then finally, looking around, as though there were road patrollers* waiting to grab her right here in my room, she said, "Oh, all right, then."

With such a serious expression on her face, I had to step on my own foot to keep from giggling at her.

"Word tell," she whispered, "that abolitionists are them that helps free slaves. Maybe they do steal some away. Don't know 'bout that. But I hear they mostly take folks up North. That's where people don't own other people like they do in the South." She thought a moment, then added, "Don't sound like evil demons to me."

"No. I suppose not." Then, waiting just the right amount of time, I said, "So, Mammy, did you ever wish the abolitionists would come and take you and Sylas away up North?"

She sighed from deep within, then sat herself down on the bed beside me.

"Missy Jane," she said. "I ain't never told you a word of a lie. And I won't now, neither. Truth is, there was a day when I did wish for that. But it was a long time ago. Back when ol' Massa, your papa's papa, was alive. He was a hard man with hard ways. This was a fearful place to be then."

She looked out at the bare dogwood limb brushing up against my window. "It was a mournful time."

"Leanna told me," I said, "that some of the slaves ran off, and when they were caught, Granpapa and Uncle Carl . . ." chewing my lip, I watched Mammy's eyes for any sign that this was going too far, "had them all whipped."

She sat quiet with a peculiar, faraway look on her face. I waited, hoping she'd say Cousin Leanna was making up one of her stories again, like when we were small, for the sheer pleasure of knowing I'd run crying to Mammy about it. I wanted her to say, "No, that never happened. Not here. Not on our land."

Her gaze was fixed in the same place as before, but I don't think she was seeing the dogwoods.

Without moving any muscle, except the angry ones in her face, she said, "I told him, you can't do it. Not now. Don't feel right to me. But they go anyway. They got caught. Ol' Massa was real mad. Most of 'em got sent to the darkest place on the whole of this earth—the Public House*—to be sold away like cattle. That's where the true demons be, child!"

"Stop, Mammy," I cried. Hearing the fierceness in her voice made my insides shake. It was as though she had a store of angry feelings that she couldn't keep from spilling out, like a too-full bucket.

"No one comes back from there. Never. They be pulled away from they families' arms. No screaming women, no crying babies can do nothin' about it. Gone. They just gone."

I threw my arms around her neck and sobbed. "I'm sorry, Mammy. I'm sorry I made you think of this. Please don't talk about it anymore."

I felt her heart pounding against her ribs. She kept breathing fast and hard, like when she's been chasing Kate's Tom* with a switch.

At last, the warm hand I've held near all my life reached up and pressed against my hair. After a moment or two, she began to sway ever so gently, back and forth, back and forth, humming the tender melody that had so often soothed me as a child.

I could have been three years old at that moment, with a skinned knee, a kitten scratch, or some silly fear. The feeling was the same. But, as always, every trace of sorrow or pain disappeared when Mammy hummed and rocked it all away.

"Hush now, child," she whispered.

Once my thoughts evened out enough to speak them, I said, "Papa should be back any time now, shouldn't he?"

"Mmm-hmmm," she said, still rocking.

"I know he'll talk Mr. Harmon into letting us buy Celia. Won't Sylas be happy, Mammy?" I pulled back to look into her face.

"Mammy?"

"Yes, Missy Jane. If Massa bring back Celia, my boy be happy then."

For just a moment, I thought I saw tears in her eyes. But then, I remembered what she always tells me: "You can't cry when there's no tears left."

CHAPTER TWO

Here Comes the Bride

When Papa returned from town, I nearly forgot about Celia altogether. Standing on the east porch, Mammy and I could clearly see that Cousin Leanna had decided to join us too. There she sat, prim and haughty, up next to our driver in the carriage.

She wore a beautiful yellow hoop skirt and crinoline* with lacy ruffles and trim. Perched on  her head was a spring bonnet, covered with silk flowers and greenery and tied fancy with pink ribbons.

A stranger looking on would never have guessed that she was only one year older than me. Because of the shamelessly grown-up way she was allowed to dress, many mistook her for sixteen—a full three years beyond what she truly was.

Mammy strolled up next to me with a fixed smile on her face. Keeping her lips as still as possible, she said, "You find me anyone in the whole Raywick County that be bold enough to wear that dress and hat so early in the season. We ain't even seen the buds of spring yet, and now we got to look at this. I don't know what kind of momma lets her child dress up in such colors before winter is done with. Where she think she is? New York?"

"Hush, Mammy," I said. "She'll hear you."

"That all right. Miss Leanna be needin' to hear *something* before it's too late." She went on huffing and mumbling to herself, knowing I couldn't miss a word.

As the carriage pulled to a stop in the yard, I stood on tippy-toe and strained my neck to see better. Leanna's personal slave, Rina, who went everywhere her mistress did, rode beside Papa. As always, she sat hunched down in the seat, as though she had no right to be anywhere that felt comfortable.

I often wished that Rina lived with us instead of with Uncle Carl's family. She looked so sad and tired all the time. I liked to wonder how it would be to see her smile.

Suddenly remembering the reason Papa had left in the first place, I took two steps down and called, "Did you bring her, Papa? Did you?"

But Mammy, determined to see that I behave properly, whapped me on the backside with her dishrag. "Whewww!" I said, laughing. I hopped down one more step.

Papa waved at me, shouting, "Well, of course I did, darlin'. Here they are."

From first sight of Celia stepping out of the carriage, it was easy to see how level-headed Sylas had lost his heart after only two months. She *was* lovely.

Her hair had been cut very short, but it still gathered into soft, light brown curls all over her head. Her skin was the rich color of polished oak, and her eyes were large and round. She wore a tattered work dress, like many slaves, but she carried herself* like a princess.

After lifting Celia from the carriage, Papa then

14

brought out a basket the size of a peddler's bag. I supposed it held her belongings. Celia took it, set it down, and tossed back the cloth covering. To my surprise, she gently lifted out . . .

"A baby!" I said. "Mammy, she has a baby."

"She surely does, Missy. That be Ruthie. Celia's sister died givin' birth to that sweet thing. So Celia took her. She be the baby's momma now. My boy say she was seven months old last week."

While Papa helped Rina from the carriage, I watched Leanna wait, distraught* over not being assisted first. She sighed loudly, on purpose, so everyone would hear. Finally, snatching the driver's hand, she let him steady her down to the ground.

Celia stood quiet, patting and soothing the baby, with a look of contentment shining on her face.

Sylas bolted from the side yard and rushed straight to my papa. He grabbed Papa's hand and shook it like it was a water pump.

"Thank you, Master Stratton," he said. "I do 'preciate this. Celia and I will never forget your goodness, sir. Why, there ain't no master nowhere that takes care of his people like you!"

"Son," Papa said, "you know we've always looked upon you and yours as our own family. With a Christian heart I could never see it any other way. Now, there is plenty to do before this afternoon comes. So, unless you intend to miss your own wedding, I suggest you stop all this chattering and see to your young lady here."

Sylas nearly hollered, "Yes, sir. Yes sir." He shook Papa's hand again and ran to Celia. Mammy walked down to meet her. Within minutes our housekeeper Kate and Mary the cook wandered out too.

Stomping up onto the porch, Leanna said, "Can you believe it?" Rina followed silently, glancing around like a scared rabbit.

Returning my interest to the people in the yard, I asked, "Believe what?"

"All this ridiculous fussing, of course. And over a slave. Some folks around here would say it's simply disgraceful."

Knowing she only wanted to start a fight, I

acted as though I was hardly listening. It usually made her furious.

"Weddings, disgraceful?" I teased.

"Well," she said, "my papa doesn't allow our slaves to marry. He says that heathens* don't understand such things anyhow."

"It's a good thing *our* people aren't heathens," I said.

She stared at me with a blank expression, one eyebrow raised. "Honey, of course they're heathens. They can't read, or write, or even understand religion. Can they? I ask you. Can they?"

I wanted to grab her shoulders and shout, "Yes! Yes, they can! All of our people can read. Most can write. Papa taught them. And as far as being religious, our workers have always been praying people. More now than ever before."

The sensible part of me knew, however, that I would not be saying anything to Cousin Leanna about people of color* reading or writing. It was, after all, against the law. That alone could cause serious trouble.

But worse yet, she had a magical way of tattling home anything that could possibly stir up her family against us. If they were to discover that just over a month ago, the Mormon missionaries had baptized all of us, including our servants— well, that could certainly bring the very walls of Jericho* down on our heads. After all . . . this is Missouri.

"Well," she went on, "my papa would never think of going to all the bother or expense of buying a slave girl and her child just to please a field hand."

Leanna pushed at the dark curls peeking from under her bonnet as if maybe one of them was brave enough to be out of place. She sniffed. "Wait until I tell Momma about all this. She will most likely faint."

Leanna buzzed on in her silly manner for such a long stretch that I found it best to think of my needlework, the new colt in the stable, or lessons from school. Anything to keep from letting her thoughtless prattle make me cross and irritable just before the wedding.

"Did you happen to notice," she said, "that your papa left me entirely abandoned on top of that carriage? But he made every effort to see that the slaves were comfortable. Even Rina. Heavenly days! What right have either of them to be escorted to safety, while I was left in peril?"

I shook my head in disgust. Then, before she could think of anything else to stew about, I moved into Rina's view and said, "Hello, Rina. How are you? I hope you had a pleasant ride."

Rina lifted her head barely enough for me to see her eyes. I could tell she'd be taking a risk to do more than nod her head a bit, but still she spoke.

"Fine, Missy Jane. I thank you." Her timid little voice always made me feel sorry.

Leanna was so used to having the stage to herself that she couldn't bear to share even the smallest corner with anyone else. She nudged Rina hard enough with her elbow to send her stumbling down two steps, then glared her down one more. There the poor girl stayed, looking at the ground.

"Leanna," I said, "what is the matter with you?"

"With me? You shouldn't be speaking to Rina

as though she were a regular person. It does her no good."

"You should be ashamed of yourself," I said. "Isn't it enough that she's always done everything you ask? Why must you keep her so frightened all the time? If you tried, I think you might even like her."

"Now see, Janey, that is exactly what I mean. People like you and your papa just run around making things difficult for the rest of us. Slaves need to be kept in their place. And besides, that kind of talk completely confuses the Negroes."

I said, "Leanna, you are awful."

My papa has tried, over the years, to buy Rina from Uncle Carl, because he can't bear to see someone mistreated so. But Leanna has trained Rina, since they were both tiny, to jump and cower at a second's notice. No, they wouldn't trade this servant for ten others.

"Jane, Jane." She shook her head at me. "Dear, you are such a child. All you think about are your silly horses and the poor wretched slaves. I assure you that when you get older and see more of the world, you will realize what matters . . . ," and she looked to Rina first, then to the servants working in the yard, "and what doesn't."

The two of us, both born with brown eyes, brown hair, and the same turned-up noses, have been called "two peas in a pod"* by the finest ladies in town. But for the last little while, it has become very clear. Our paths are no longer going the same direction. I do believe each of us is determined to hold our ground.

True Ties

Sylas and Celia were married in a lovely little ceremony beside the grape arbor* at four o'clock that very afternoon. Squire* James, a good friend of Papa's for years, came to perform the marriage. He and the Mormon missionaries who had taught us the gospel were the only guests we invited from town, as there are few people that will support this kind of thing these days. The squire pronounced the two man and wife, and then Old Mac, Mary Cook's husband, not being one for too much seriousness, recited a few stirring verses to the newlyweds from Job* chapter three. Something about misery and darkness. I suppose that was his idea of the joys of marriage.

Before he had finished, the workers and wedding company were in stitches.*

Papa stepped to the porch and hushed everyone up.

"As you all know," he said, "it is our custom to give the new couple a fair start with two hens, a rooster, and their own cow."

Papa motioned for Brewster, the stock hand, to come forward. He sauntered in, bowing and tipping his hat like he was the lead in some kind of parade. Old Mac and the elders pushed him forward so everyone could get a better look at the new milk cow and the spindly calf that trotted behind her.

Skipping after his pa was eight-year-old Kate's Tom, carrying a squawking burlap sack.

Brewster handed the cow's lead rope to Celia. She nodded graciously, then smiled as Kate's Tom tossed the chicken bag at Sylas.

Everyone cheered and clapped for the couple, while Mammy stood by holding and loving little Ruthie. It was easy to see she was happy with her boy and his new family. Everyone was—well, *almost* everyone.

From the upstairs window, Leanna glared down on us with the same cross look her momma always wore.

Gazing up at the guest-room window just as Leanna ducked behind the curtain, Squire James said, "Robert, how do you explain the incredible difference between you and your brother, Carl? The two of you—and your families—couldn't possibly be more different."

"The two girls were nearly raised together, you know," Papa said.

Squire James tapped his pipe on the porch rail. "Doesn't matter," he said. "Jane is kind and even tempered and a mirror of her mother's beauty." Leaning over to me, he whispered, "A bit too taken with fast horses, I hear . . . but nevertheless, a fine young lady."

I felt my cheeks blush, but I didn't mind.

"Then you take that ill-tempered little vixen that keeps poking her nose out the window, though she won't come down here and be civil. She's just like her daddy, that one."

"Yes," Papa said. "I'm afraid you're right. It's a

shame, too. She is such a beauty. Though we rarely see her smile."

The bride and groom stood off to the side of the crowd, whispering and giggling. If anyone tried speaking to either of them, they seemed not to hear at all but held on to one another as tightly as they might if they were near a cliff.

After Squire James left, I took Papa's arm, and we walked through the long, green stretches of lawn and down toward the orchard. In just a month or so, the trees would be covered with pink and white flowers.

Tipping my head back, I closed my eyes and tried to remember that sweet smell of apple blossoms. In my mind, I could almost hear the bees buzzing over us.

"Where have you gone, Janey?" Papa asked. He pulled my hand farther through his arm and patted my fingers.

"I'm still here," I said. "Papa, won't it be wonderful to have a baby around our place again? It's been years and years since we've had one to look after."

"That's true," he said. "Will you mind Sylas

not being around so much? He's nearly been a big brother to you."

"Well, I admit, it is hard for me to watch him behave in such a peculiar manner. I'm used to his calm, sedate* ways. But he is carrying on like a crazy man. Is this what falling in love does to people?"

Papa smiled.

"Ah, Janey," he said. "I suppose it's quite normal for new married couples to stand around grinning like utter fools. We'll allow them happiness, won't we? I dare say they'll find their senses again soon enough."

He stayed quiet for a while, looking over the land. It reminded me of the times when he and my momma went for long evening strolls together. I loved to see them, walking arm-in-arm through the apple trees. Mammy would shoo me back from the window, saying, "Let those lovebirds alone, child. They don't need you nor anybody else spying down on 'em."

Papa must have been thinking same as me.

"Do you remember," he said, "how your mother used to adore these parties? Why, she'd plan for days to make sure that everything was just so. Helping Cook and Kate make spiced cakes and ginger punch. All of us would end up scurrying here and there to finish up whatever needed doing. What a time she'd have."

"I do remember," I said. "She made a flower wreath for my hair and a bouquet for the bride. Once I even got a new dress."

"Your momma did enjoy making things special," he said, turning his face away. "She was like a white magnolia blossom. Lovely and fragile."

How he missed her.

I recall my momma as a pale, soft-spoken, delicate lady. It seemed that any outing which took much work or travel would certainly bring her down to her sick bed. Mammy and the other house servants would end up tending to her, sometimes for a month, until the color came back to her cheeks.

I wasn't usually allowed to see Momma if she was very sick, so when they called me upstairs to her room, three years ago last November, I bolted up, thinking she was finally getting well again. No one prepared me to see her looking so gray and thin and tired. It was plain she was slipping away from us. I held on to her tiny white hand until its warmth was gone.

Being so young, I didn't know how to watch her die. After they sent me out of the room, I recall jumping on my pony and racing madly through the orchards until a low, outreaching branch brought me down. It's a wonder I wasn't killed. Curling myself up in the tall, cold grass, it seemed as though I cried . . . forever.

Old Mac told me years later that just before dark Mammy walked right to the spot where I was, as if she'd known all along where to find me.

She says she had an impression,* and just went to where she felt I was at. They say that she carried me all the way back to the house by herself.

Mammy talked sweetly to me that night, saying my momma had gone back to Jesus but that she was leaving behind a special angel to watch over me. Mammy has held on to me ever since, like she was that angel.

Papa and I didn't come in until early candle-light,* and most everyone had wandered back to their own cabins. I was just think-ing how nearly perfect the day had been. Papa had decided to stay up a while read-ing his new Dickens novel, so I closed the door to the drawing room.*

Upon reaching the bottom of the stairs, I heard Leanna stomping down, then saw Rina cowering behind.

"Jane Stratton," Leanna said at about the fifth step, "I've been waiting all afternoon for you to come inside. I've never been so neglected in all my life."

"Leanna, you should have come out to the party. We had a wonderful time. You would have enjoyed yourself."

"I can't imagine how. But never mind all that. I need a word with you and your father. Immediately." She walked right past me, pushed on the drawing room door, and started in.

"Fine, then," I said. We probably looked like a children's parade, marching through on Papa that way. He acted startled, but I just shook my head and shrugged.

"Uncle Robert," Leanna said. "There is a serious problem which you are perhaps not aware of. I am just sickened to be the one to bring this to your attention, but there are some things you need to . . ."

"Leanna, please," Papa said, trying not to appear irritated. "Tell me what the problem is."

"Well. As I was saying, you need to know that after all you've done to show your slaves . . ."

"I'm sorry," he said. "We don't call them slaves here."

"What *do* you call them, then?" Now she was the one acting bothered.

"Usually, our people, our workers, or by their names."

"After all you've done to show . . . *your people,* then . . . kindness, they have in return betrayed you."

Papa's eyes grew stern, but my stomach hurt.

"In what way, may I ask?"

"While resting upstairs, I sent Rina out to

fetch me a drink. After nearly shriveling up waiting, I went to see what had happened to her.

"I heard voices coming from another room, so I stopped to see who it was. There, sitting as calm as you please, was one of your servants and a child. I asked her name but she didn't answer me. In her hand, though she tried to hide it, I found . . ."

Leanna motioned to Rina, who pulled a small brown book from her apron pocket and reluctantly handed it to her mistress.

"This!" she said, with a strange air of satisfaction.

I closed my eyes in disbelief, praying that when I opened them again, this would not be happening.

"As you can see, it says Book of Mormon."

Neither of us needed her to say what it was. Yet when I heard the words, my heart jumped so hard I caught my breath. The little book had been given to us by the missionaries when we were baptized. Papa told our people that he'd keep it in his study. Anyone was welcome to read it in their spare time, on one condition. To avoid problems, they must take pains* to stay out of sight with it. Especially if we had guests who fretted over Mormons.

Mammy came past the door, looking as fearful as I felt. She motioned for me to come out, but my feet wouldn't move, so she pulled the door shut. Papa stared at Leanna, no doubt vexed that this spoiled child had such power to throw our household into turmoil.

"Do you understand what this means, Uncle Robert?"

Papa said nothing.

"Not only did that girl bring this devilish book into your house, but she appeared to be *reading* it—which is against the law, as you know. If this wicked slave has been listening to those Mormons . . . well, you should have her whipped. I know my pa would be more than happy to do it for you. Why, he says that Mormons will all be run out of the state and that everything they own should be burned."

Papa looked as though he would explode with anger. But when he spoke, somehow he kept his voice steady. "Perhaps you have done what you considered to be your duty," he said. "But may I remind you that you are a guest in my home? How I deal with this matter is no concern of yours—or your father's."

His tone startled her, I could see. I'd never been so proud of my father. The control he used while dealing with such an awkward situation was amazing.

"Of course, Uncle Robert," Leanna said. Then, stepping toward the fireplace, she held our book, our precious book, over the flames. "At least we can be done with this vile thing," she said . . . and let it drop.

"No!" Papa shouted. Rushing toward the hearth, he grabbed through the flames. The book had just begun to smoulder as he snatched it out and smothered it against his dress coat. Turning it over, he patted the singed cover and glared up at Leanna.

"Uncle Robert," she said, "why would you ever . . . ?"

"This is *my* book," Father said, through

33

clenched teeth. He brushed at the soot and charred corners.

Exactly when Leanna and Rina ran back upstairs, I don't know.

Papa took down a small carved box from behind the atlas. He opened the lid and set the scorched book down gently among a stack of curious square papers. He then closed the box and put it back in its bookshelf hiding place.

As I watched Papa close the box, I noticed a streak of raw, red skin along the side of his hand and wrist.

"Papa, you're burned."

Without much thought, Papa turned his hand over to look. "It's nothing," he said.

"What do you think Leanna will do now?" I asked.

"Honey, we couldn't rightly send her home without a good story to tell, now could we?"

He teased, but I could see he was fearful for our servants, especially for Kate . . . and for all of us.

CHAPTER FOUR

Joining Up

To our utter shock, after Leanna went home, we heard nothing from her or her family, nothing at all. It was unlike them to let even one day go by peacefully if any fuss could be made. Finding Kate and her son reading the scriptures had to be the worst scandal yet. How could Uncle Carl resist the perfect chance to cause such a stir? Leanna had lit out of here like her dress was on fire, so naturally we expected the worst. When it didn't come, we offered grateful prayers.

Before the morning birds awoke, Papa had Sultan harnessed, saddled, and working down the highway into town. The elders had sent word the previous day that they had an urgent matter to speak to him about. They hoped to see him at his earliest convenience. That was why he left before sunup.

Most of us in the house were still asleep when Papa left. But he'd been so full of anxious excitement that he had rattled throughout the place half of the night. At the first hint of color in the dawn sky, he was out and away.

I awoke fully some hours later with a warm ray of sunlight streaming over my feet. The smell of bacon, bread, and hominy* seemed to slip under my door, calling, begging me to come out after it.

By the time I had splashed cold basin water onto my face, I had to dress quickly or shiver  myself silly. Mammy always fretted so over my hair. But I simply pulled and twisted it into a chignon* and covered the bun tight with a silver net.

If I could busy myself downstairs before Mammy discovered I was awake, I stood a small chance of escaping the brush ordeal.

Careful to avoid every creaking board, I tiptoed lightly past Mammy's room and toward the stairs. Just as the point of my slipper touched the top step, Mammy's door swung open. It startled me so that I nearly took a tumble down to the parlor.

"Don't be thinkin' I can't see you, Missy Jane," she said. "Go on, then, child. Go on with your hair lookin' like a horse's tail. I'll catch up to you soon enough. And when I do . . ."

Taking the steps two at a time, while she talked on and on, I was soon out of earshot.* Into the kitchen I rushed, snatching a piece of hominy and tossing it into my mouth.

Cook turned from her bacon and, with half a smile, held up the cooking fork in a most threatening manner. "Out now," she said. "Out! I didn't hear no voice calling you down here to torment me. When I say this meal is ready, it be ready. Now get!"

"I'll go. I'll go," I said. Then swinging back around, I asked, "Is Papa in from town?"

"Ain't come yet," she said. "Massa told me, 'You just keep them vittles pipin'* and I'll be there to see 'em gone.'"

"Then I think I'll wait for him on the porch."

"Not without your shawl, you ain't." She

pulled the wrap* around me, saying, "Mammy mighty liable to beat me if you catch a chill in this morning air."

"Mary," I said, "the sun is getting warmer every day."

"That don't matter. You keep it on."

Old Mac stood crouched over on one foot, tugging off a muddy boot. As I came through the door, he grinned kindly up at me.

"Morning, Missy Jane." He nodded.

"Morning, Old Mac."

"That new colt of yours is looking strong. His ma don't want me messing with him just now, but I got me a chance to walk him 'round while she was eating. His legs is straight and his back is fine. Someday he carry you high and proud."

"He is beautiful, isn't he?" I said.

"That he is, Missy."

"Old Mac?"

He kept his eyes down on purpose, so he didn't have to look me in the face. But he knew exactly what I was after.

"Yes'm?"

"Tell me. Do you think . . . I mean . . . will he be . . ."

Old Mac shook his head, laughing, and said, "I know what you want. You say, 'He pretty horse, shore enough, but Old Mac, I jest wanna know. Is he goin' be . . . is he goin' be *fast?*'"

"Well, I must know. Do you think he will?"

"Heh, heh, heh," he laughed. Then, working the other boot off and dropping them both in the mud corner,* he decided to end my suspense.

"Yas, Missy Jane," he said, coming close to my face. "He goin' be fast like lightnin', that one. Why, folks won't see you two comin' this way or goin' that. He be lightnin' for shore."

From the kitchen, Cook called out, "Old man. Don't you be helping that child. Her head already too full of shoutin' and horse riding, and *doin' up her own hair.* She like to be a fine lady someday. That is, if there's still time to save her."

I bit my bottom lip, giggling, and made for the door. Old Mac waved me out, saying, "I'll smooth her down.* You go on."

It took no waiting time at all. Before I could set myself into the Sleepy Hollow,* Papa came

39

galloping through the yard. He swung his leg over the saddle and slid down, all in one motion. His expression was deep and thoughtful, as always. But when I met his eye, he broke out in a wide grin.

He held a letter bunched in one hand as he ran up the steps.

"Honey," he said, "this is the answer to our prayers."

I had no idea what he was talking about.

"Which prayers, Papa? That the apples will grow red and firm? That Leanna and her family

will go to China, and like it? That Mammy won't make me work on that wretched sampler one more day?"

Mammy came from the side yard and heaved herself up to the porch. Her face was set in a shiny, round scowl.

"What that you saying 'bout me? You should be tellin' your pa what a sinful child he has. You should be tellin' him how you sneaked away from me when I was hollering. You should be tellin' him how you be running out here before you fixed up right and presentable. Don't be talkin' about me when you the one bein' wicked!"

"Mammy," I said, changing the subject, "Papa has some news to tell us."

"If you two are quite finished," he said, "I do have something to say."

"Sorry, Papa," I said.

Papa sat down on the seat beside me and cleared his throat.

"This is in answer to our prayer of 'What ever shall we do when we're found out?' Perhaps Leanna hasn't worked on her parents sufficiently to bring them here. But we both know that in time she will. They'll have the cavalry camped on our doorstep before too long. We must have a plan of escape, and I believe we've found one."

"Escape? Papa, really," I said.

"Darling, once it is made known throughout the county that we are Mormons, it could become very difficult for us here."

Actually, I had thought of that. But as frightening as it was to imagine folks wanting to do us harm over our religious views, I hadn't really figured we'd have to leave.

Papa spread out his papers.

"This is quite a lengthy letter, so I will tell you the gist of it.* First off, it is from Salt Lake City."

Most of the Mormons had moved west to a new land called Salt Lake. But it was on the other side of the world from us. Well, nearly. How could they possibly know anything about Papa?

"Directed to you?" I asked.

He nodded. "It's a marvel, isn't it?"

"Oh, Papa. What does it say?"

He raised his eyebrows to quiet me. "It says, among other things, that in view of the difficulties which are now threatening the Saints in these parts, we are requested to join with them in Florence, Nebraska, by June ninth of this year. We will there ready ourselves for the journey across the plains to the valley of Zion."*

I found no words to speak on my tongue, in my mind, or within my heart. Zion? Wasn't it out in the wilderness territory somewhere? This was a surprise, to be sure.

After one look at Papa's face, there was no doubt in my mind. We would be going.

CHAPTER FIVE

Answers

"So . . . you can't say for sure when you'll be back?" I stood behind Papa as he finished tying his bedroll to the back of Sultan's saddle.

"By the middle of next month, for certain," he said, patting my face. "But, you never know, Darlin'. If all goes as planned, I could be home much sooner."

"I hope so," I said.

Papa had agreed to travel back with Sylas and the elders as far as Council Bluffs.* He was thinking that they could make many of the arrangements for us from there. He had learned that much help was needed to plant crops for the Saints who migrated through the settlement on their way west. He figured to arrange for our future and then come back to sell the plantation and outfit us for our journey.

"Honey," Papa said, "Why are you fretting over this? I have been away on business many times before. And often for much longer."

"What if Leanna finally works her folks up enough to . . ."

"Now, I've thought of that. So I sent word just yesterday to Squire James in the form of a letter. He knows the whole story and is on our side. I asked him to look in on you every few days. He will see to it that you are taken care of until I return. Besides, Carl's business is with me. If he finds that I'm gone, he will just have to go home and wait. Won't he?"

"I suppose."

"Our workers will take care of the orchards and the crops. They have been running this place since before your Momma and I were married." Then laughing, he added, "Why, this should point out quite clearly who is needed here, and who isn't." I wrapped my arms around his waist and hugged him.

"We need you, Papa."

Celia and Ruthie were standing back by the cabins with Sylas. I suppose the first time a couple is separated, they take it the hardest. He gave baby Ruthie a kiss on the forehead, then said something sweet to Celia and held her tight. Taking up her hand in both of his, he gently kissed her fingers.

Celia touched the corners of her eyes with her apron. It seemed a very tender moment, so I looked away rather than intrude upon it.

Still holding on to Papa, I said, "Perhaps I'm having one of Mammy's impressions. I'm worried that something will happen to you."

"Don't you even think such a thing. I'll be back, just as I said. Nothing is going to happen to me."

He tilted my chin up just enough so that there was no escaping his gaze. "You're my little blossom. You know that. How could I not come back soon? I love you so."

"And I love you, Papa."

He and Sylas mounted their horses and shouted their good-byes to everyone. Mammy made Sylas get back down to give her a kiss.

Finally they were on their way. I'd have waved my hankie at them, but there wasn't one in my pocket.

I couldn't get a grasp on what this feeling was supposed to mean. It was like planning an enormous picnic knowing all along that the storm clouds were gathering. Something was coming.

We waited for Squire James to drop in on us after a few days, but he didn't come. Everybody knows that judges are very busy men, so we figured he was tied up in court for now.

Sitting around doing nothing has always given me the absolute fidgets. Brewster knew that, so he took me riding. He tried to let me choose whatever horse I wanted, but Mammy caught us. She saw to it that I was carefully placed atop one of the oldest nags we have. I may as well have been given a plow horse. And before I could escape, Mammy tied a bonnet on my head. At least we were able to get outside in the fresh air for a few hours.

It would have been more to my liking to pull

away and race through the south field with the
wind chilling my face and knotting up my hair.
But since I didn't want to have Mammy mad at
Brewster or cause my old horse's death, I decided
to just go at a trot.

"Brewster?" I said.

"Yes, Miss Jane?"

"Why is Mammy so afraid to let me ride the
fast horses? I'm careful. Papa even lets me sometimes. I'm nearly thirteen years old. Why does she
still fuss over me so?"

He thought for a long time before saying
anything.

"Miss Jane. It's true that your pa likes to keep
the hard world away back from his child. Ain't
that so?"

"Well, yes."

"It's because he loves you, and don't want
nothing making you sad or bringing you harm.
Mammy feels that way too."

"I don't understand. Why does she . . ."

"That's right," he said. "You don't understand.
I reckon, though, that it's time you did." He loos-

ened the reins and let his horse nibble at the pasture grass.

"Mammy may not be the oldest of us folk, but it don't matter none. She's been there an' back.* You understand what I'm sayin'? Those eyes have seen more than the rest of us want to."

"You mean when Grandpapa and Uncle Carl ran this place. Don't you?"

"Yes'm. Your daddy was a child. He always be gentle and kind to us. But he was the only one. Now, Mammy had her a husband named Isaac. Hardworking man. They had them five young'uns. One time he nearly cut his whole thumb off wood chopping. Ol' Massa whopped him good for making himself half a thumb. He decided to escape. Some others reckoned they go too.

"He say to Mammy, 'Corinne, honey. I'm tired of this life here. I'm gonna make my way north to freedom. Then I'll come get you and the children free too.'

"She was 'bout to let him go, but she got one of her 'feelings,' real strong. She beg him to stay. But he don't.

"Massa caught him. Then he was real bad off. Next we know, all the runners sold away, and 'cause Isaac was the leader, Mammy's five babies get sold too."

"Oh, Brewster," I whispered.

"Massa took 'em to the Public House Auction,* and sold 'em off like they's pigs or chickens. Mammy took sick and near died of a grievin' heart. Six months after that she give birth to Sylas. Years later, your momma pass on from this life and give her *you*. She needs to take care of someone. Her boy and you, Missy Jane, ease up her sorrow some."

I knew that anything I said would come out all rattly, so I stayed quiet. Just as we came up to the barn, Brewster said, "She already lost so much, child, she can't think 'bout losing no more."

We put the animals away and got them settled. Coming out of the barn, I said, "Thank you, Brewster. I had no idea."

"It was time, that's all."

Mammy met us before we got close to the house. I wanted to stand back and look into her eyes. Forever, I'd see her differently, and it made me feel as though I could understand some of what was locked up inside her.

She was already chattering to Brewster. "This very bad. I knows it now."

"What is?"

"This sense I got. It's bad."

"Mammy, I've been feeling that way too," I said. "Like something awful is coming. It's one of those impressions. Isn't it?"

"I don't know, but I's worried sick."

"Mammy, we just have to think about this . . ."

She stopped a few paces behind me. When I turned around to see why, she had her mouth open and was pointing to the road.

A fancy carriage was just pulling to a stop in front of the house. Sitting tall, with their noses held high in the air, were Uncle Carl, Aunt Alice, and Leanna.

"Oh, no," I said. "We have to move fast! Brewster, send Kate's Tom after Squire James. Then go around back and get Kate out of the house. You set her up in one of the far-back cabins. Tell her she *must* stay out of sight. Now, hurry!"

"Yes'm."

"And Mammy, try not to look so nervous. It will be all right, I tell you."

I wasn't at all used to ordering the servants around, but under the circumstances, it was better than standing around acting edgy.

Mammy was talking to herself again. "No, child," she said, clutching her apron. "This ain't no impression . . . this a bad dream."

CHAPTER SIX

Thin Blood*

I wasn't sure whether or not Uncle Carl and Aunt Alice were expecting me to rush up and greet them. Any other time, I would have given them a polite hug and peck on the cheek. Unless, of course, they had come in a rage over some silly report from Leanna.

I remember the fit they threw when Papa decided to grow up orchards and corn instead of cotton. Shouts of "Traitor!" could be heard clear into town. No one in their right minds would have approached them then.

This time, it felt uncomfortable just to see them, especially after the way Leanna had left. Heaven only knows what she'd told her parents about Kate and the book. I never thought trying to act normal would be so hard. Before I had an etiquette* decision to make, Aunt Alice came forward and, taking both my hands, pulled me to her and kissed my cheek.

"Dear, dear Janey," she said. "It is so wonderful to see you again. My, don't you look lovely."

To say she was acting unlike herself was putting it lightly. Knowing how Aunt Alice enjoyed having tantrums, I had expected her to start right off by scolding me, as she always did, for the riding calluses on my hands or my sun-chapped face. When she pretended not to notice, I was at a loss as to what to do.

Uncle Carl acted first and bowed like a gentleman. "Miss Jane," he said, touching his hat. That really made me jumpy.

"And Corinne, how nice to see you," he said, turning to Mammy with a smirk.

I understood now why Mammy had always acted like something in her was boiling over whenever he came around. She refused to look at him but said simply, "Mister Stratton."

This polite game seemed harder for Leanna to play than anyone else. After her momma fired

three or four side jabs her way, she finally curt-
sied. I did too.

How could I possibly act normal if they were
going to be so odd? Why were they not angry? I'd
prepared to say, "Papa's gone, you'll have to talk
to him later," but Papa's whereabouts didn't come
up.

We walked them into the parlor and Cook
(taking Kate's usual place) took their wraps and
made them comfortable.

Mammy and I tried to appear calm, though in
our minds we were wringing our hands and pac-
ing the floor.

My aunt and uncle exchanged glances, then
both began to speak at once. After a bruising look
from his wife, Uncle Carl let her take the reins.

"Janey, darling," she said, "would you be so
kind as to tell your father that we are here. Tell
him we won't keep him long because we have
other pressing matters to attend to."

I confess that my next thought was, *Good, they
will be leaving soon.* But I was still having trouble
figuring out why they were being so nice.

"Janey?" she said.

"Yes, ma'am?"

"I asked you to please go get your father."

I looked to Mammy for help but got none. Realizing that I was pretty much on my own with this, I gave my planned speech.

"I'm sorry. He's not here. You will have to come back another time."

Leanna nodded to her papa in a primpy way. He raised both eyebrows and turned to Aunt Alice.

She pursed up her lips and made her eyes nearly disappear. I stared for a minute to see how she did that, but I couldn't tell. She should have been flying around like a mad chicken by now, but instead she stayed calm and asked, "My dear, where has he gone?"

"He is out of town on, umm, business."

Now all three of them exchanged looks. I felt like the only one in the room who didn't know what was happening. Why didn't they just ask about Kate's reading the Book of Mormon, so I could tell them they must wait for Papa?

"Business?" Leanna said. "That's not what I heard."

Now, Leanna's sassy mouth I recognized.

Before I had a chance to plan my words out calmly, I heard myself say, "And just what did you hear, Miss Troublemaker?"

Mammy pinched my arm. But I already had my hand over my mouth. It didn't help. I shouldn't have said that. Honestly, I didn't want to know what she had heard. I only wanted to hear the door open and find Squire James or, better yet, my papa standing there.

Aunt Alice gave Uncle Carl a nod so he'd know he was allowed to speak.

"We have heard," he said, "though I'm certain it was a misunderstanding, that your papa is getting mixed up with those Mormons."

He leaned forward and looked straight at me—hard.

"Some folks in town," he said, "tell us that he has actually *become* one of them. They say that not too long ago, he abandoned you all here and has gone to join with them."

I wanted to slap his face. But I'm certainly not that brave.

"He didn't abandon us . . ."

As though he had not heard me, he said, "Now, of course, I wouldn't easily believe my own brother would do such a thing. But, having seen the true nature of Mormons, I know they are capable of anything. It would help if you could tell us exactly where your papa went."

I clenched my teeth together and said nothing.

"Perhaps you don't realize the danger your father could be in."

"What danger?" I said.

"This country is full of marauders.* They rob and kill people every day. And they don't like Mormons. Why, a man was found dead just last week on the road to Iowa."

I gasped without meaning to.

Uncle Carl smiled and let me know I'd given him the answer he was waiting for. Then he continued, "For all we know, it could have been your dear father. You just might be an orphan already."

I saw the room getting blurry. *It wasn't him, it wasn't him, it wasn't him, it wasn't him,* I chanted in my mind. Anything to drown out that dreadful voice.

"This is Missouri, girl! We have already . . ."
He stopped, closed his eyes, and began again.
"*They* have already run those people out of here
before. Don't imagine they won't do it again."

The sleeves of my dress were sticking to my
arms. Why was he talking to me this way? I
wanted to cry out that I was only a child. What
did he want me to say? I couldn't separate one
thought from a dozen others, but finally I man-
aged to blurt out, "I told you, my papa isn't here.
You'll have to talk to him when he comes home."

"Fine, fine," Uncle Carl said. He leaned back
and crossed his ankle over his knee. "We'll just
have to do our best to take care of you while he's
away. Won't we?"

Both Aunt Alice and Leanna smiled, but their
eyes were as dull and grey as stones. I felt my
whole body tremble as though an icy wind was
blowing around my feet.

Uncle Carl went on. "We have other things
that we can talk about. Leanna tells us that you
have a colored woman here who likes to read. Is
that so?"

I flashed a glare at Leanna with such fire that

for one small second she looked afraid of me. It didn't last long enough.

"Well, no matter," he said. "She will turn up soon enough. I know how to take care of slaves who cause trouble on my place."

"This isn't your place." I knew better than to speak to an adult this way, but the words came out before I could catch them. And I wasn't sorry.

He clenched his teeth for a moment. Then, throwing back his head he laughed husky and loud. "Of course you're right, dear," he said. "For now, at least."

CHAPTER SEVEN

Thick Water*

By week's end, it became plain as day that Leanna and her family weren't going anywhere. They helped themselves to every part of our home and began looking upon the rest of us as intruders. They talked to me pleasantly enough at first, though I had little or nothing to say in return. But as time wore on, they found it easiest to ignore me altogether.

Kate's Tom returned to his pa with the report that there was no one in the office of Squire James. Hearing that sent a cold chill up my back. Papa had said the Squire would check on us every few days. Where could he be?

Once the family had taken over the upstairs, I no longer slept in my bedroom but stayed with

Mammy. I expected Aunt Alice to make me stop talking to our workers altogether. But she didn't seem to care. While Aunt Alice and her family weren't kind to them, it surprised me that they weren't cruel either. My brain worked night and day trying to figure out what my relatives were up to.

One afternoon, I sat with Mammy and the others outside of Old Mac's cabin. We had started meeting there sometime each day, everyone except Kate, of course, who stayed out of sight. Suddenly, Cook came bustling out of the house toward us like a frightened rabbit. She still had a duster in her hand, and she glanced around behind her every few steps.

"Missy Jane, you don't know what they sayin' in the Big House* now. We in a fix, for sure."

"What is it?" I said.

"I be cleanin' all around the place, and I come up on the family. They be talkin' real loud like they knew you was gone. I didn't mean nothing, but I hear Miss Leanna say, 'I's tired of taking care of myself. Rina should be doing it, Daddy. How long we got to act all syrupy nice like this?'

"Then her momma say, 'That's right. You got to take care of them soft slaves* so's we can *get our own.*' Then," Cook gulped air and kept going, "Mister Carl, he say, 'You know I can't do that without first I get Miss Jane outta here.' What we goin' do? Miss Jane, they goin' sell us off!" She grabbed up her apron and started to cry.

No one said a word, but as I searched each face, it became clear that with Papa gone, our workers were waiting—waiting for me to say or do something that would make everything all right. The trouble was, I'd been so taken care of all my life that I had no earthly idea how to deal with something this big.

Instinctively I looked to Mammy. On her face I saw none of the panic that the others wore, but rather an icy defiance that made me feel stronger somehow.

"What shall we do, Mammy?" I asked. "If Papa was back . . ."

Through clenched teeth, she said, "We got to get you outta here, Missy Jane."

"I can't leave you," I said, expecting that to be the end of it.

Suddenly she stood, staring down at me.

"Hear me now, all of you," she said. "This a bad day, I know. We all scared. But we made a promise to Massa Stratton to take care of his child. I know the good Lord 'spects us to keep our word. We goin' to do it, like we said we would."

Everyone nodded but me.

Trying to protest, I said, "But I won't go . . ."

"You hush now, child." Mammy snapped. "We got no time for this foolishness."

Taken aback by the harshness in her voice, I looked away, feeling tears well up in my eyes.

Mammy's face softened as she reached out and gathered me in her arms. "Miss Janey," she said softly, "The day your sweet momma passed on, she handed you to me and she said, 'Take care of this baby, Mammy. Keep her safe. She's yours now.' I have loved you and done for you the very best I ever knew how. Now you got to do as I say, because . . ."

Her voice quivered, and for the first time I could remember, there were tears running down her face. She began again.

"Because ain't nobody taking one of mine from me. Not again. Not ever again."

Celia stood and held Ruthie tight in one arm, with her other arm around Mammy. Mammy finally straightened up and took charge. With only a second to think, she said, "Brewster, you send Kate's Tom after the squire one more time. Then you hunt out a hiding spot for Missy Jane."

"Yes'm," he said, running to get his son.

Next, she said, "Old Mac, you get on whatever horse is left in the barn and head up north to Council Bluffs. You gotta find this child's daddy. Got to. You know them finger pointers,* so you don't get too lost."

"I'll do it, Mammy," Old Mac said. "Now, you know the road is full of patrollers jest waitin' to catch an ol' slave with no papers. I'd stand a better chance of makin' it through if I had me a pass."

"He's right," she said. "Miss Janey, you've got to work us up a travelin' pass. I don't write so good, and he better have one, else he's gonna be caught for sure."

"I can do it, Mammy."

"It's the most hope we got, child." Turning back to the others, she said, "The rest of y'all go 'bout your work. Folks in the Big House can't know what's going on out here."

Without too much fuss I was able to take Papa's inkwell and pen holder from his desk in the study. I ripped a blank page from his memorandum book* and a page with his signature on it. Seeing our current situation, I knew he wouldn't mind. On my way out, I glanced up at the atlas, wishing there was time to snatch the Book of Mormon and take it with me. But if anyone was to find that now . . .

We sat in Mary Cook's cabin to make up the paper, because the sun shone in better there than anywhere else. My hand shook so badly, I ended up writing four different passes before we got one near perfect. It read,

> *Allow my man to pass through to Council Bluffs, Iowa.*
>
> Robert Stratton

We gave it to Old Mac, and he quickly stuffed it into his pants pocket.

"Take Missy Jane's horse," Mammy said, tossing a sideways glance at me. "From what I hear, he's the fastest."

"Yes'm." Then, twisting his tattered hat in his hands, he said, "But now . . . what if he ain't there? What if he *is* . . ."

I knew what he was thinking, and it made me sick inside and mad at the same time.

But Mammy got to him first. "Don't you be saying nothin' like that around here. Sylas is there too. You put the fright in Miss Jane or Celia and I'll whop you myself. Go on, now, and bring Massa home. Go!"

"Yes'm," he said, running for the barn. Within minutes he was tearing down the back road, heading north.

"Please, Lord," I whispered. "Bring back Papa."

Mammy took my hand in hers and squeezed it tight, saying, "Amen to that."

CHAPTER EIGHT

Hidden Away

Uncle Carl's family carried on, being civil to the workers and trying not to notice me. If I hadn't known that they were trying to send me away, I no doubt would have stepped into a trap. As it was, all three of them tried to talk me into outings of every sort, simply to get me into the buggy. A morning ride, a picnic, a trip into town. Each time I had an excuse that exasperated them, but one they couldn't argue with. But I knew that my stomach aches and school work would not hold them off too long. They were running out of patience, so I knew we were running out of time.

All while I was stalling, Brewster worked on my hideout. Mammy said we needed to be ready at a moment's notice for when I couldn't put them off any longer. I was to say, "Let me just get my parasol," then rush to the cabins. It worried me to wonder what they would do when I didn't come back. We never got the chance to find out.

Uncle Carl came in from town one afternoon while I was out back with Celia and the baby. Celia wrapped Ruthie in a shawl and scurried off the minute he pulled in.

He had taken the wagon, which was so unlike him. He is more the new-buggy type. With a forced politeness that tensed the muscles in his face, he said, "Janey, honey. Come here. I have a surprise for you."

Knowing the way he used words to say something different than they meant, I didn't smile, nor did I come any closer.

Raising his chin to an odd angle, he glared at me, "I said *come here.*" He stood swatting the riding crop against his black boots as if he hoped to feel the pain as it struck his leg.

Taking one step toward him, I stopped.

"Consider my surprise, Miss Jane," he said, "upon learning that a slave from this farm was caught wandering around somewhere up in Iowa country. And with a badly forged traveling pass. Now what do you think he was doing up there?"

My head jerked in the direction of a woman's scream coming from the front of the house. What was happening? I felt sure it was Cook's voice, though I'd never heard such a sound. I wanted to run to that voice—and run from Uncle Carl—but I was too afraid to move.

He kept whipping at his boots, faster and faster, coming nearer to me with every few strikes.

"You realize, of course, that we can't have this kind of thing going on around here." He had the look of a wild man. "I will not . . . put . . . up . . . with . . ."

Never in all my life had I been more than scolded for upsetting Mammy. And now that real danger was upon me, my mind somehow didn't accept it. I had no clear thought as to how to save myself or that I needed to, for that matter.

And then I found that some reactions are not planned. As Uncle Carl raised his arm, I fell to the ground and curled into a perfect cocoon, with my hands tightly wrapped over my head. I waited for the blow, but it never came.

Amid the crying in the front yard there came a different sound. It was the shrill, angry voice of Aunt Alice calling, "No, Carl, no! There's a better way."

I could still hear his labored breathing, but that soon faded and the other sounds trailed off. I finally dared to peek in the direction of my uncle. He was just entering the house as I looked up, and he did not look back at me. Aunt Alice was chattering crossly at him as they disappeared into the house.

My body felt heavy and lifeless, as if I'd taken sleeping powders.* As much sense as it made to get up and run to the cabins, still I lay there unable to move. I knew, though, that for a few minutes or for a long time, depending on my aunt's mood, she would demand Uncle Carl's full attention as she berated him and insisted that *her* plan—whatever it was—was better. The smell of the grass took me back to the wedding day . . . and my walk with . . .

"Papa," I cried softly. "Papa."

A light touch on my hair made my whole body jump. Brewster's large, gentle hands slid under my back, lifting me up and carrying me away. The next feeling I had was of being settled down upon a straw mattress.

"Thank you, Brewster," I heard Mammy say.

Her soothing fingers stroked the hair from my face as she said, "Can't no one hurt you now. Mammy's got you, child. You safe now."

"Celia, you got to get a poultice* to Old Mac now. My Missy Jane be scared past herself, and I need to stay with her."

All the voices drifted off as I slept. I dreamed of floating, small and helpless, wrapped first in Momma's arms, then Mammy's. I imagined a baby whimpering softly, and horses flashing like wind-blown sparks through the night sky. On the largest and fastest one rode my papa, coming to send the darkness away.

"Mammy say you got to wake up now, Miss Jane."

No, I thought. *Not yet.*

"She say you got to wake up."

Recognizing Celia's voice, I tried to stretch.

My shoulders ached, but seeing Ruthie on Celia's hip made me sit up and reach for her.

"No time for that now," Celia said. "Mammy says you got to be awake and ready to get going when she comes back. *Those people* be looking for you."

That woke me up. I pulled my dress and stockings on as quickly as I could. I had to ask her a question, even though I feared the answer: "What happened to Old Mac? I heard the crying. Is he . . ."

"No," Celia said, "he ain't dead. The patrollers caught him. They saw that he got papers on him, all right. But the patrollers say the papers be no good. Old Mac told Mammy he was mighty close to where your papa was when they got him. He had just enough sense to chase your horse down toward the Bluffs camp. He say, 'Tell Missy Jane I's so sorry.'"

I buried my face in the bed and sobbed.

"Then Papa's not on his way? He doesn't even know we need him? I should never have let Old Mac go. This is all my fault."

Mammy hurried through the doorway. "We

72

gotta get you outta here, Missy. We got to go now."

Wiping my arm across my eyes, I followed her outside. The sun hadn't been up for too long. Some of the roosters were still crowing. I said I wanted to see Old Mac, but Mammy said, "That won't do nobody no good."

Once we got out past the barn, if I said even one word to Mammy, she shushed me. We walked through the tall, misty grass until my shoes were soaked and the hem of my dress hung cold and wet with dew. Coming at last to the back few rows of apple trees, I was tired and soggy and ready to stop. But Mammy motioned me forward. We turned right at one point and kept going through the orchard. My side ached, and still we walked. Finally, we stopped.

"Thirty trees back. Eighteen over," Mammy said.

"What?"

"This here be your hideout, Missy. Brewster and his boys fixed this place for you in the night."

If Mammy hadn't stopped and pointed the spot out to me, I would have missed it altogether.

What appeared to be a pile of branches and leaves was really a little shanty* made from old boards. It was low enough to the ground and covered over with so many tree limbs that Mammy had to show me how to go inside.

"Honey," she said, "We stored food and blankets in there for you. Now stay put till I come back. We told the family you just ran off, probably to one of your many friends around about the countryside, and don't nobody know to where. That should keep 'em busy for a while anyway."

"When will you be back?" I asked.

"By nightfall, I hope."

"But what if . . ."

Mammy put her soft hands on each side of my face. "Don't know 'bout any ifs, honey. But you got to stay safe. Can't nothing happen to you. That's all. You hear me?"

My eyes burned, and it hurt to breathe.

"I love you, Mammy."

"I love you too, child."

CHAPTER NINE

Ticking Clock

By nightfall, I had both blankets wrapped around my shoulders and still my teeth chattered in the cold. I sat inside the shelter making puff clouds with my breath, but it didn't help distract me. How I wished I'd taken the wooden box when I had the chance. The little brown book would have brought me such comfort. It would have been a little piece of Papa that I needed now.

I kept trying to convince myself that Mammy would be here anytime and tell me what to do. But the darker it got, the less I believed it. Every night noise startled me so that I finally gave up watching for her and settled deep down into my little hole. Any sleep that came was fitful. I kept imagining that I heard voices, or crying, or some-one's footsteps coming nearer.

By morning I dared to wander out and hide myself behind the trees, closer to the house, because I supposed that if Mammy did come to find me, I'd see her first. After waiting for what seemed like hours, I knew something must have gone wrong. She would have sent someone out with a message or some help—unless there was trouble.

Crouching in the tall orchard grass, I waited for the first sign of anyone who could tell me what was happening. No one came to work in the garden. The cows were still in the barn, bawling to be milked. There was no one washing win-dows, beating the parlor carpets, or scrubbing the porch. Where could everyone be?

Just as the stillness of the yard had me believ-ing I was the last living soul on earth, I saw from the distance that the front door of the Big House was opening. But disappointment hit me hard. Instead of someone slipping out to my rescue, Uncle Carl and his family walked toward a wait-ing buggy.

On her way down the stairs, Aunt Alice

screeched something into the open door, and my heart skipped. That had to mean that someone, one of our people—maybe Cook or Celia—was inside!

It was terribly hard to stay put until they finally rode out of the yard. I watched them disappear into a cloud of dust before I made a move. Then, dashing from the orchard, I sped past the silent cabins and around the dogwoods and thundered up the porch steps. With the enemies gone, I felt safe pushing open the front door and rushing in. Closing it behind me, I leaned back to catch my breath. I heard footsteps coming from the hallway.

"Cook?" I said, "Celia?" But there was no answer. Just as I turned to run back out, I heard a timid voice.

"Miss Jane? You can't be coming in here now."

"Rina!" I couldn't believe my eyes. "What are you doing here? Where is everyone else?"

She came closer and whispered, "Your people ain't here no more. The workers in this house been brought over from my massa's place. You best get outta here, Miss. Anyone sees you and it'll go bad. They been lookin' for you all night.

Massa brought field hands to burn all the trees
down, in case you in there."

"Burn the orchards? Why?"

"I hear Miss Leanna say your daddy ain't coming back, so her daddy goin' burn all those trees
and grow cotton, like this land is meant for. Go
now, hide yourself . . . before they catch you."

She started pushing on me before I even had
the door opened.

"Wait," I said, taking hold of her arm.
"Where is Mammy? Where are Celia and the
baby? Rina, listen. I have nowhere to go. Can't
you tell me what's happened to Mammy and the
others?"

She hung her head down as if Leanna was
standing next to her. "I told you all I know! Miss,
you gotta go before they find you."

"All right. All right. But there is something
you can do for me."

She had that cornered-mouse look in her eyes
again. "What?"

"Make sure no one comes toward the drawing
room. There's something I need."

"I'll try, Miss."

Tiptoeing around the corner and into Papa's study, I had no trouble finding the atlas. I pushed a chair against the shelf and grabbed down the box. The chair wobbled just enough to shake my balance, and in catching myself, I dropped the chest. It hit the side of the desk and fell to the carpet.

I heard one of Aunt Alice's servants yelling down the hall, with Rina saying something about books falling. Knowing someone could come in at any minute, I snatched up everything that had fallen and stuffed it back into the box. The square papers were getting crushed, but it didn't matter. The noises outside the door stopped. I waited, hoping Rina would find a way to let me know when it was clear.

Lifting the lid off the carved chest, I shook it gently to settle the things inside. The Book of Mormon had survived the shock well enough, but some of the papers were rumpled and creased. I smoothed out two or three before seeing that each one was a note signed by Papa. I took as many as I could find and stacked them together. I glanced over them, and a few words nearly came off the page.

I, Robert Stratton, declare this day the said slave Brewster to be a Free Man.

Signed, Robert Stratton

Tears came to my eyes as I read the names on each one: MARY COOK, OLD MAC, KATE, CORINNE . . . There were even two new papers for Celia and the baby. It was just as Mammy had told me: our people were not truly slaves at all. They had been free for years, but they chose to stay with us. Now what had become of them?

Rina knocked lightly and opened the door. She stood twisting her apron in her hands, frightened for me.

"They went upstairs, Miss. You got to go. Please. They'll be coming back to this room any minute."

I held the papers up for her to see, but she

looked away. "Do you know what these are, Rina?" I cried.

"Naw, Missy," she said. "I don't read."

"These are freedom papers! That's why we never called our workers slaves. They *weren't* slaves. Rina, can't you tell me? Where have they gone?"

"They in the darkest place. It's too late to help them now."

Grabbing her shoulders, I breathed, *"Where are they?"*

Rina pushed a folded piece of parchment across the floor with her foot. "Take this. Please, go." Her voice quivered. "Please." After slipping the freedom papers into my pocket, I grabbed up the Book of Mormon and the parchment and ran outside.

PUBLIC AUCTION

SLAVES TO BE SOLD.
FINE NEGRO MEN,
WOMEN, & CHILDREN

RACE COURSE GROUNDS
WEDNESDAY, MARCH 30TH 1859 10:00 A.M.

Today!

Running to the stables, I grabbed a fistful of mane, pulled myself up onto the first horse in the stall, and galloped away. Barreling out onto the lane in front of the stables, I saw smoke coming from the far end of the orchard. I brought the horse to a dead stop. It was true, then. Uncle Carl must know somehow . . . Papa wasn't coming back.

I wanted to sink down into the earth and let it cover me over. But the thought of Mammy in the place she feared most shook my senses back to right.

Perhaps the workers inside the house could see me from the window, or from the doorway, or from a crack in the wall. I didn't care. There was no one else to save Mammy, Celia, Old Mac, and the others—the only *real* family I had. No one else but me.

CHAPTER TEN

Worth of a Soul

The clock had already struck eleven by the time I left the house. My only hope left was that I wasn't too late.

When I arrived at the race course, I found it easy enough to mingle in as though I belonged with one family or another. Moving from stall to stall, I searched desperately to find anyone from our place. But I saw only subdued, sorrowful-looking men, women, and children huddled in horse sheds with no furnishings, not even tables or chairs. Some were eating rice and beans and a bit of cornbread, but unless they wanted to sit in the mud, they ate their food standing up. Many of them gathered into sad little groups that looked around fearfully at the rest of us.

I could faintly hear what was going on within the main building, and after finding none of our people outside, I knew that I must go in. Taking a deep breath, for courage, I headed straight  toward the main door, as if I knew what I was doing. Such a large crowd had gathered around the entrance to watch the slave auction that I couldn't see inside. And there was no way for me to get in without calling too much attention to myself.

There were very few women here and no other children that I could see, except those being sold. This dreadful place seemed to belong entirely to Southern men.

Supposing myself to look like a poor street child, what with my dirty face, mussed hair, and tattered dress, I hoped they would ignore me completely, as busy people often do. "Pardon me," I said, in my most ladylike tone. But no one even turned. Waiting for that one perfect chance, I finally saw a gap in the logjam of onlookers and pushed my way through it.

Certainly every kind of human being imaginable was in this auction area. One side of the building was open completely to the air, and the race course could be seen beyond. On another wall a platform had been built, about two feet high, where three important-looking men sat at desks keeping the record books. A slave stood on the platform while buyers in the audience called out their bids.*

The room was so full that I had to stand in one place and turn slowly to make sure to see each and every face clustered around the sides.

Suddenly several cries came from behind the platform as a short, stocky man pushed a woman and child forward. The woman was *Celia*. Before I could make a sound, I was swept off the floor. I screamed, "Put me down!" He held me tightly around the waist, saying, "Oh, no you don't, Missy!" Though I couldn't see his face, there was no mistaking Uncle Carl's angry voice. "I've been waiting for this day for far too long to let you spoil things now."

After dropping me out the back door, he brushed the dust from his clothes and ordered, "See that this orphan beggar doesn't come in here disrupting things again!" Without so much as a glance at anyone, he marched back inside. A large man nodded and grinned down at me.

"I'm not an orphan," I said to him. "I must go in. He's trying to sell people who are already free!"

"Is that so?" the man said, blowing cigar smoke straight at me. "And just who do you suppose I'm gonna believe—a fine gentleman like Mister Stratton, or *you?*"

"But, sir, I have their papers here." Taking the wrinkled notes from my pocket, I held them out to him.

He was more than happy to snatch the stack from me and pretend to read them. Then, glaring down, he said, "That's the beauty of our fair state. The law says that for a slave to be free, he has to carry his papers with him—at all times! If he don't have them, then he ain't free. Looks like these ain't no good, doesn't it?"

He took the cigar out of his mouth and held the smouldering end to the papers.

"No!" I yelled. "Give them back!"

There are times when it is no use to struggle and there is more sense to walking away defeated.

But there are other times when it makes no difference whether you see winning or losing ahead. You must fight anyway. This was one of those times.

I made a furious swipe for the freedom papers just as the corners began to smoke. He just laughed and waved them over my head.

Knowing that this dreadful man held the very lives of my beloved "family" in his filthy hands, I stepped outside myself and found a piece of courage I didn't know was there. Leaping forward, I grabbed onto his arm and bit into it with all my might.

He let out a yell that silenced the crowd outside the building. People turned to stare as he stood rubbing angrily at his wound. Realizing that all eyes were now on us, he made a feeble attempt to smile, though his eyes were still blazing furiously.

Without looking behind me, I scooped up the notes and pushed my way back inside. No one paid me any mind as I ran from one man to another, attempting to explain. Finally I reached the recorder's desk and spread the papers over his ledger book.

"Please sir," I said, "this woman and her baby cannot be sold."

He looked up and tugged at his spectacles.

"They don't belong to anyone," I cried. "They're free. These folks behind you are all free."

The recorder stood and shouted to the auctioneer, "Hold up a minute! We have a situation here." He climbed to the podium and in a loud voice said, "This child says that these slaves do not belong to anyone, but are in actuality freemen. Can anyone justify her claim?"

Uncle Carl glared at me in a most threatening manner but remained still.

Just then a voice in the back called out, "I certainly can!" and the stately figure of Squire James appeared. My knees weakened as the most powerful man in the county came forward and took me into his arms.

I stood beside him as my uncle pushed forward and the two had words.

"I have every right to sell these slaves! They

possess no papers. My brother Robert has abandoned his estate and is most likely dead."

"No, no! He isn't dead!" I shouted, praying all the while that what I said was true.

"And that makes her an orphan, and Robert's estate mine," he said, smirking. "And I do not free my slaves."

"It just so happens," the Squire said, "that I have a letter clearly stating Robert Stratton's intentions to come home and remove his family out west. He certainly has not abandoned anyone. And you, sir, should be arrested for attempting to sell what does not belong to you."

Turning to the constables who were now inside the room, he said, "Gentlemen, see that this man is detained."

A week later, Squire James sat on the veranda* sipping cool lemonade with Papa and me. "That's a brave little girl you have there, Robert," he said.

"Yes," Papa said, smiling, "I've often worried that she was perhaps too brave for her own good. But now I see that she has wisdom beyond her years as well. I'm so proud of her." He brushed my cheek with the back of his hand. Just days ago, I thought I'd never feel this touch again.

Squire James bought our house and property outright. Said he always did love the place, and he promised to replant the trees that were burned.

The money from the land made it possible to buy four wagons, along with mules, horses, oxen, and all the provisions we needed to begin our  journey west. Papa said that if all went well, we'd be gathered with a large group of the Saints by mid-August. We rode out of this country smiling. Sylas, Celia, Mammy, and baby Ruthie took the lead wagon. Old Mac and Mary Cook came next in the second. Brewster, Kate, and Kate's Tom followed behind them. Papa and I came last, with Papa seeming almost like a shepherd bringing in his sheep.

And Rina, Leanna's *former* slave, with her crisp new freedom paper folded into her pocket . . . well, she sat next to me. Her smile was the most beautiful thing I'd ever seen.

I remember Papa saying, "I've always looked on our people as family. With a Christian heart, I could never see it any other way."

Me neither. After all, the way you treat people in this life is all that really matters. Isn't it?

GLOSSARY
In Janey's Own Words

abolitionists—People who are against slavery. Some were known to help slaves escape from their cruel masters. Other times they provided a hiding place for the runaways. See page 4.

been there and back—Old Mac meant that Mammy had lived through a great many terrible sorrows. See page 50.

bid—The price someone is willing to pay for something at an auction. See page 89.

Big House—The house that the master and his family live in. See page 63.

boar brush—A hairbrush made out of the stiff bristles of a wild pig. See page 1.

candlelight—The time of evening when the sun goes down and we need candles or lanterns to see by. See page 29.

cannibals—People who eat other people. Canada was a place where many slaves ran to be free, so to frighten slaves and keep them from escaping, their masters told them that the Canadians would eat them. See page 5.

carried herself—Moved and acted in a graceful way. See page 14.

GLOSSARY

chignon—A twisted knot of hair at the back of the neck, held fast with a net. See page 37.

Council Bluffs—A small town on the Iowa side of the Missouri River. Most of the Saints who journeyed to the Salt Lake Valley began from this pioneer settlement. See page 45.

crinoline—A full, stiff underskirt. See page 12.

Deep South—The area well known for having the harshest laws on slavery. The Deep South included the states of South Carolina, Georgia, Alabama, Mississippi, and Louisiana. See page 5.

distraught—Upset beyond repair. See page 15.

drawing room—Short for *withdrawing room*. A place where the men could be alone to discuss important matters without being disturbed. See page 29.

earshot—If you are *within earshot,* you are in a place where someone else can hear you. See page 38.

etiquette—A fancy way of saying *good manners.* See page 55.

finger pointers—Signs on the roads to tell a traveler which way to go. See page 66.

freedom papers—Legal note from the owner of a slave giving him his freedom. See page 6.

gist of it—The main idea. See page 43.

grape arbor—A shady trellis covered with grapevines. See page 22.

heathens—People who have no religion or don't believe in God. See page 16.

hold herself in—A person who doesn't *hold herself in* is not afraid to say whatever she thinks. See page 6.

hominy—Boiled and treated corn kernels with the outer skin removed. See page 37.

impression—A good feeling or a warning from the Holy Spirit. See page 29.

in stitches—Laughing very hard. See page 22.

Jericho—A city in the Bible which was crushed when the walls around it fell down. See page 18.

Job—A book in the Bible, well known for its sad story of a man who lost everything he loved. His life was only misery. Not the ideal thing to read at a wedding. See page 22.

Kate's Tom—When two people are given the same name, we use nicknames to keep from being confused. My papa's given name is Thomas Robert Stratton, so when Kate named her son Tom, we called him *Kate's* Tom. See page 10.

Mammy—A former slave who helped my Papa raise me after my momma died. See page 1.

Massa—The master of a plantation—in this case, my papa. See page 3

marauders—People who hid out on the roads to rob travelers. See page 59.

memorandum book—The book Papa kept his financial records in. See page 67.

mud corner—A place to drop dirty shoes or clothes. See page 40.

people of color—Black people from Africa. See page 17.

persimmon-puckered—Making a sour face at someone. You just can't help but pucker your face when you taste a bitter, nasty persimmon. See page 6.

pipin'—Steaming hot. See page 38.

polecat's meanness—If someone has a polecat's (skunk's) meanness, they're so mean that you avoid them like you would the stink of a skunk. See page 5.

poultice—A thick, soothing mixture of herbs on a cloth. It helped cuts and bruises heal faster. See page 74.

powders—A doctor's medicine to help you sleep. See page 73.

Public House—An auction place. See page 9.

road patrollers—Men whose job it is to catch runaway slaves. See page 7.

sedate—Calm and peaceful. See page 26.

shanty—A poor person's house. See page 76.

Sleepy Hollow—A comfortable chair like the type that Washington Irving, a famous author, sat in to write. He wrote "The Legend of Sleepy Hollow." See page 41.

smooth her down—Make her calm again. See page 40.

society—The higher class of people, the ones who have education and money. See page 2.

soft slaves—Servants who are used to being treated well. Too well, in the opinoin of Uncle Carl and his family. See page 64.

sorely done to—Treated very badly. See page 6.

squire—The town judge. See page 22.

take pains—Go to a lot of trouble. See page 32.

thick water—The saying "Blood is thicker than water" means that family ties are stronger than friendships. In my case, it was just the opposite. I was closer to our workers than to my uncle's family. See page 62.

thin blood—See *thick water*. Meaning the feeling I had for my Uncle's family was not a good strong one. See page 54.

two peas in a pod—When two people are just alike, we say they are like two peas in a pod. See page 21.

veranda—A large porch. See page 94.

wrap—A coat or shawl. See page 38.

Zion—Where people who are trying to live the gospel are. Or the Salt Lake Valley, far away in Utah Territory. See page 43.

WHAT REALLY HAPPENED

Quite a few people who lived in the southern states were converted to the gospel of Jesus Christ. Many of them owned slaves. The Church encouraged its members to treat all men fairly, but these converts were not forced to free their slaves. To their credit, most slave owners, after joining the Church, did give their workers freedom. Many former slaves chose to stay with the families they worked for out of love and devotion. Some even traveled west and settled in the Salt Lake Valley, adding greatly to the cultural diversity and rich heritage of the area.

ABOUT THE AUTHOR

Launi K. Anderson grew up in Los Angeles and San Diego, California. After moving to Utah, she worked at Deseret Book stores in Salt Lake City and Orem for four years, including a year as a children's book buyer. She loves historical fiction and enjoys the research as much as the writing.

Launi lives in Orem, Utah, with her husband, Devon, and their three daughters and two sons. She loves music and spends some of her happiest hours listening to her husband and children play the piano, violin, and flute. Her hobbies include flower gardening and collecting creamers and great quotes. Her favorite things are history, cats, family, parties, people, and the sound of wind chimes. In her ward, she has served in the Primary, Young Women, and Relief Society and is currently second counselor in the Primary presidency.

She is the author of six other Latter-day Daughters books: *Clarissa's Crossing, Maren's Hope, Ellie's Gold, Violet's Garden, Gracie's Angel,* and *Hannah's Treasure.*

"Father, do you think I'm ugly?" I hadn't meant for the words to come out sounding so full of hate, but they did.

Father put his finger beneath my chin and raised my head. "Caroline," he said in a voice most sincere. "You are the most beautiful thirteen-year-old I know. You look much the way my mother did when she was younger."

I looked at the portrait of my grandmother on the wall near the fireplace. "She doesn't look knobby," I said.

"What?" Mama asked. Her voice went squeaky at the end.

"I mean," I said, trying to think of a good word—one Mama would think acceptable—"she doesn't look too, uh, lean. She appears to have . . . meat on her." Grandmother Gallagher was beginning to sound a little like a chicken right before dinnertime.

Father smiled and glanced at Mama, his eyebrows raised a tiny bit. "I think you'll be needing a talk with your mother soon."